A TEXT MESSAGE FROM THE HEART

Written By:
Nia Olivia Lindsey

ISBN: 978-0-578-58784-4

Inquiries should be emailed to:
ATextFromTheHeart@gmail.com

DEDICATION

To God. “I can do all things through Christ.”

To my mom Eleanor (Ellie) for always sending me love wherever I am...from her heart to mine.

To my Dad, Donnie, and my brothers, Trey and Warren. I’m so blessed. I will always have three men who love me and always have my back.

To all my family and friends. I love you.

“It’s time to get up!” said Mommy.

Nia did not move.

Then Mommy kissed her all
over her face.

"I'm kissing you up!" said Mommy.

She gave Nia a big hug and kiss.

Nia giggled.

Nia got up and quickly put on her school clothes.

It was the 100th Day of School!

Nia was so excited on the 100th Day of School.

She could hardly eat her breakfast. Nia wanted to go... NOW!

At school, everyone had to decorate a hat.

Some students decorated their hat with 100 of their favorite things.

Each student also had to bring 100 pieces of candy.

HAPPY 100th DAY OF SCHOOL
100
100
100
We've been here 100 days!
100
I am 100 days smarter
100
100

HAPPY 100th DAY OF SCHOOL
100
100
We've been here 100 days!
100
100
100
100

They made a 100th day stew with all the candy.

Everyone got a big bag or bowl of candy to take home.

There was even a cool 100th day cake! Yummy!!

SCHOOL
100
We've been here
100
days!
100
100
100
100
100
100

Then, the students marched around the school waving their 100th Day of School flags.

Some students put 100 stickers on their flags.

They all had so much fun!

After all the
100th Day fun
and a good lunch,
it was time for
a nap.

As Nia was falling asleep,
she thought of her Mom.

At that same time, her Mom was thinking about her.

Her mom was saying, “I hope Nia is having a good day. I love you sweetheart.”

Then suddenly, Nia felt a warm and tingly feeling.

When Mom picked Nia up from school, Mom asked Nia about her day.

Nia told her about all the fun things they had done to celebrate the 100th Day of School!

100

Mom said, “I wish I could have been there, but I thought about you so strongly.”

Then, Nia jumped up and said, “I felt your love Mommy!”

“It was a text message from your heart!”

A TEXT MESSAGE FROM THE HEART

CPSIA information can be obtained
at www.ICGtesting.com
Printed in the USA
BVHW022020310120
571011BV00013B/13